W9-BDJ-826

This Golden Book belongs to

_____

_____

My Christmas Alphabet

Photos by Claudia Kunin

A GOLDEN BOOK · NEW YORK
Western Publishing Company, Inc., Racine, Wisconsin 53404
Packaged by the RGA Publishing Group, Inc.

© 1993 RGA Publishing Group, Inc. All rights reserved. Printed in the U.S.A. No part of this book may be reproduced or copied in any form without written permission from the publisher. All trademarks are the property of Western Publishing Company, Inc. Library of Congress Catalog Card Number: 93-70099 ISBN: 0-307-13720-1   A MCMXCIII

Aa angel

In the Christmas show at school, I was dressed as an **angel**

Bb bell

I rang a Christmas **bell**, too!

Cc cookies

On Christmas Eve, Mommy and I make a plate of **cookies** to leave for Santa.

Dd decorations

I put Christmas **decorations** on the tree and all around the house.

Ee elves

Santa has little helpers called **elves**.

Ff feast

On Christmas Day, Mommy and Daddy fix a big Christmas **feast**. Yum-yum!

Gg garland

We decorate the table with a **garland** of fir branches.

Hh holly

Holly is a plant that is red and green—
the colors of Christmas!

Ii icicles

Icicles twinkle in the light and make our Christmas tree sparkle.

Jj jack-in-the-box

Surprise! I unwrapped a present, and a **jack-in-the-box** jumped out!

Kk kings

When Baby Jesus was born, three **kings** traveled from far away to bring him gifts.

Ll lights

Colored **lights** shine brightly on our Christmas tree.

Mm mistletoe

When I have **mistletoe** over my head, I get an extra Christmas kiss!

Nn nativity

Our **nativity** scene shows Baby Jesus lying in the manger.

Oo ornaments

We make **ornaments** for our tree.

Pp presents

We make our own Christmas **presents**, too!

Qq quilt

On cold winter days, I like to snuggle with my grandma under a warm Christmas **quilt**.

Rr ribbons

We wear pretty **ribbons** in our hair at Christmastime.

Ss stocking

On Christmas morning, my **stocking** is full of surprises!

Tt tree

Our Christmas **tree** is an evergreen. Mommy says it reminds us of everlasting life.

Uu underwear

When it's cold during
Christmas, we wear
our long **underwear**!

Vv vests

My sister and I have **vests** to wear on Christmas Day.

Ww wreath

Our Christmas **wreath** is almost as big as I am!

Xx xylophone

One of my Christmas presents was a **xylophone**.

Yy yule log

Daddy brought home a big log to burn in the fireplace on Christmas Day. He calls it a **yule log**.

Zz zoo

One of my presents on Christmas morning was a little **zoo**. Merry Christmas to me!

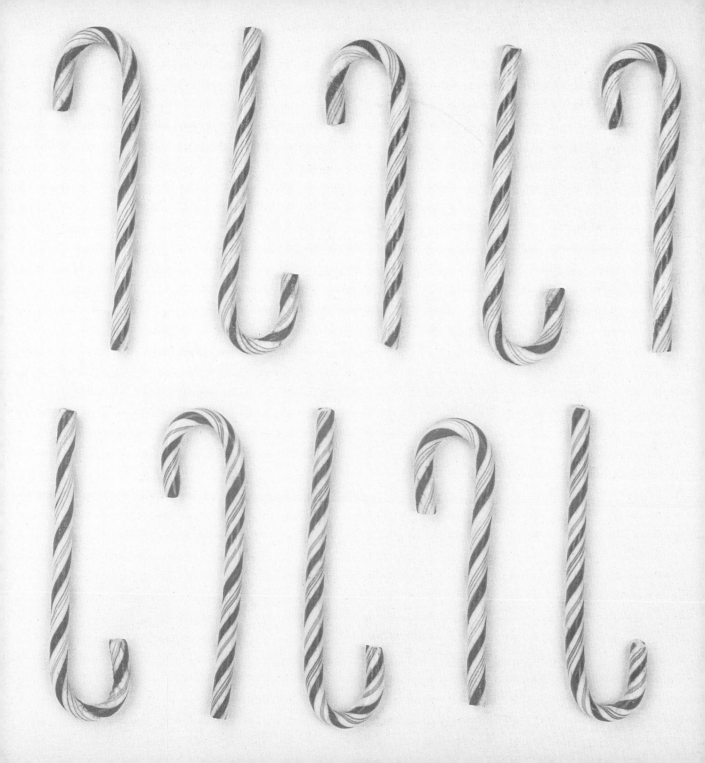